MARC BROWN

Arthur's Promise

Arthur ran home from school as fast as he could
to catch a brand-new episode of Bionic Bunny.
But when he got there, D.W. was already watching TV.

"Arthur, guess what!" D.W. said excitedly. "There's a
Mary Moo Cow Special coming up next. 'Mary Moo
Cow Meets the Rainbow Pony!'"

"No way, D.W.," said Arthur. "It's time for Bionic Bunny."

"I'm allowed," said D.W. "Mom said so."

"Please," Arthur pleaded. "I'll buy you a new coloring book if you let me watch my show."

"Nope," D.W. said firmly.

"How about a coloring book and new crayons!"

D.W. shook her head no.

"Okay," said Arthur. "What will it take?"

"There's only one thing I want," D.W. insisted. "And that's to come to your next Bionic Bunny Fan Club Meeting."

Arthur was desperate. "Okay! Just let me watch my show!"

"Is that a promise?" D.W. asked.

"Promise," Arthur replied.

When the big day arrived, D.W. ran to find Arthur.
"Grandma made me a Bionic Bunny costume to
wear to the meeting!" she said.

Arthur couldn't believe his eyes. He would have to do something before D.W. embarrassed him in front of his friends.

Arthur tried to talk his parents into taking D.W. to the zoo. "I heard the ape family has a new baby," Arthur explained. "D.W. will love her!"

"Sorry, Arthur," said Dad. "Your mother and I are too busy today."

Arthur even called Grandma Thora. "Can you take D.W. to the park today?" he whispered.

"I would," she said. "But isn't D.W. going to your club meeting?"

Arthur checked the time. The meeting was at three o'clock. He had to think fast.

First he pulled out all of D.W.'s Crazy Bus videos. Then he gathered her favorite toys and put them on the couch. He popped in a video and took a deep breath.

"Hey, D.W.!" Arthur called. "Your Crazy Bus video is on."

"Gee, thanks, Arthur," D.W. said.

Arthur waited until D.W. started singing along.
Then he tiptoed out of the room.

Arthur ran to the tree house to change into his official Bionic Bunny
T-shirt. But when he got there, D.W. was waiting for him.

"Surprise!" D.W. cried.

"Oh, no," sighed Arthur. "I'm too late."
Now he was stuck with D.W. *and* his promise.

D.W. heard a noise.

"Somebody's coming!" she said.

"Bionic Bunny forever!" shouted Buster.

Arthur felt doomed.

"What's she doing here?" asked Buster.

"Well…" Arthur stammered. "You see…she…"

But before Arthur could think of anything to say, Binky, Francine, and the Brain climbed up into the tree house.

Francine pointed to D.W. "What's *she* doing here?"

"I'm here," D.W. said sweetly, "because I know a lot about the Bionic Bunny."

"Oh, yeah?" Francine said. "Like what?"

"Well…" D.W. began. "I know how much the Bionic Bunny loves double chocolate brownies!"

"Wow, D.W.!" Buster exclaimed. "What else do you know?"

"I know how much the Bionic Bunny loves sugar cookies," D.W. said.

"Cool, D.W.!" Binky remarked. "What else do you know?"

"I know how much he loves Bionic Berry punch with rainbow sherbet," said D.W.

"No way," said Francine. "That's my favorite!"

"Oh, boy!" Buster exclaimed. "This is going to be our best meeting ever!"

Later, over dinner, D.W. told her parents all about the meeting. "I even got to learn the secret Bionic Bunny handshake!"

"Maybe for your next meeting, I can make my carrot layer cake with creamy mayonnaise frosting," said Dad.

That night, at bedtime, D.W. went into Arthur's room.
"Since everybody liked having me so much," she began,
"maybe now I can come to all your club meetings."

Arthur rolled his eyes.

"I saved you a Bionic Bunny brownie...." said D.W.

"Well," Arthur replied. "Maybe one or two more meetings
would be okay!"